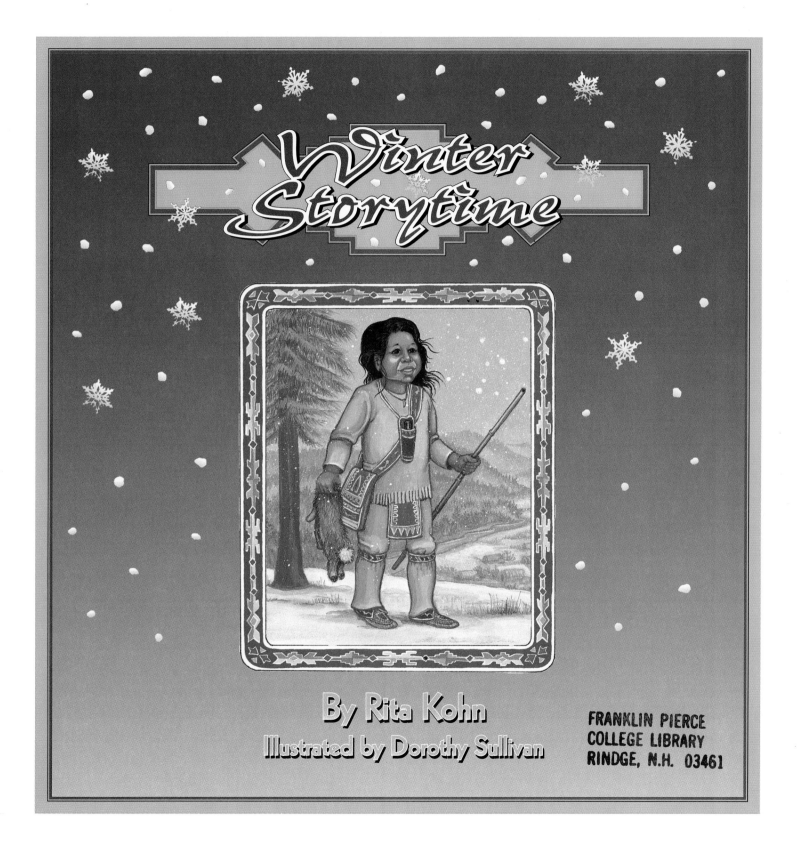

Winter Storytime

By Rita Kohn
Illustrated by Dorothy Sullivan

The Woodland Adventures series
is dedicated to all the Woodland People
who persevere despite hardships, inhumanity, and hostility.
Their spirit, like the Eagle, soars.
Their integrity, like the Turtle, persists.

This book is dedicated to
my Mother and Father
who settled in the Catskill Mountains (the stony country)
between the Hudson and Delaware Rivers,
where I roamed and absorbed the stories
in the stones, the trees, and the sky.

Special thanks to:
Wap Shing, spiritual Leader of the Miami of Indiana,
and to my Consultants
Curtis Zunigha -- Lenape (Delaware) and Isleta Pueblo,
James Rementer -- Community scholar for the Delaware of Eastern Oklahoma,
Tom Stephenson -- Delaware of Eastern Oklahoma,
Gwen Yeaman -- Chippewa/Penobscot,
Robin McBride Scott-- Cherokee,
and Beth Kohn, Early Childhood Specialist

Library of Congress Cataloging-in-Publication Data

Kohn, Rita T.
        Winter storytime / by Rita Kohn; illustrated by Dorothy Sullivan.
            p.   cm. -- (Woodland adventures)

    ISBN 0-516-05204-7

                1. Delaware Indians-- Folklore. 2. Winter --Great Lakes Region --
Folklore. [1. Delaware Indians -- Folklore. 2. Indians of North
America -- Great Lakes Region -- Folklore. 3. Folklore -- Great Lakes
Region. 4. Games -- Folklore.] I. Sullivan, Dorothy, ill.
II. Title. III. Series
E99.D2K65 1995
    793 -- dc20

                                                                94-38377
                                                                CIP
                                                                AC

Text copyright © 1995 by Rita Kohn
Illustrations copyright © 1995 by Childrens Press®, Inc.
All rights reserved.
Published simultaneously in Canada.
Printed in the United States of America.

1 2 3 4 5 6 7 8 9 10 R 04 03 02 01 00 99 98 97 96 95

Project Editor: Alice Flanagan
Design and Electronic Production:
    PCI Design Group, San Antonio, Texas
Engraver: Liberty Photoengravers
Printer: Lake Book Manufacturing, Inc.

The Purpose of This Book

Winter Storytime, one of four books having a SEASONAL theme in the Woodland Adventures series, is a picture book for preschool and primary grades based on learning SEQUENCE such as long ago, now, first, second, third, and fourth.

The story takes place in the winter in a woodland region along the Great Lakes of North America, the traditional homeland for more than twenty NATIVE AMERICAN nations. It is a retelling of a LENAPE (LĒ NĂ´ PĒ), or Delaware Indian, traditional tale of how the first "kokolesh" (rabbit-tail) game was made. The game came to be played during the winter months when children amused themselves indoors while Elders worked inside the lodges.

In this story, children listen to grandmother tell her two grandchildren the story of how the original kokolesh was made and learn the significance of traditional values such as respect, inventiveness, problem-solving, and transmitting cultural ways.

"Look!"

cried Molly,
"It's the first snowfall."

"First snow!" said William.

"That means it's storytime!" said Mollie.

William jumped up
and down with excitement.

"Story, story," he cried.

William and Mollie

ran to the kitchen
where grandmother was waiting.

They gave her a big hug
and snuggled up to hear
the first story of the winter season.

Grandmother smiled.
"I am going to tell you a Lenape story of how
the rabbit-tail game was first made.
We call the game 'kokolesh.'
My grandmother told me this story.
She heard it from her grandmother, who also
heard it from her grandmother."

"A long
time ago,
the Lenape lived
in the mountains between
two rivers that flow
into the great ocean.

They told a story
about Little White Wolf
and how he came
to make the first
kokolesh to play with.

It happened on the day
of the first snow.
Everyone was busy
making things.

9

Grandmother was making a basket.

Mother was making
a rabbit-skin robe
for the coming baby.

Grandfather was
making a pipe.

Father was
making a cradleboard.

10

'I have nothing to make,'

said Little White Wolf.

'You can help me,' said grandmother.

'You can
help me,'

said mother.

'You can help me,'
said grandfather.

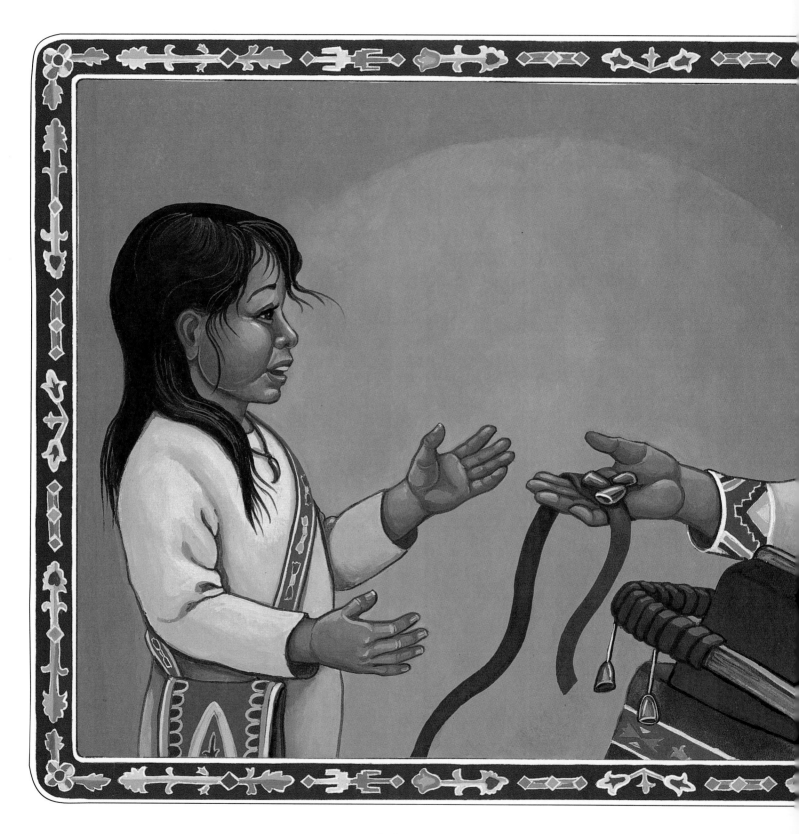

'You can help me,'
said father.

Little White Wolf
looked around.

**'I want
to make
something
to play with,'**

he said.

From grandmother

he got a leather string.

From grandfather

he got a sharpened stick.

From mother

he got a rabbit's tail.

From father

he got three cone-shaped
bones from deer toes.

First,

he tied one end of the leather string
around the rabbit tail.

22

Second,

he strung the cones on the leather string.
All the larger openings of the cones pointed
away from the rabbit tail.

23

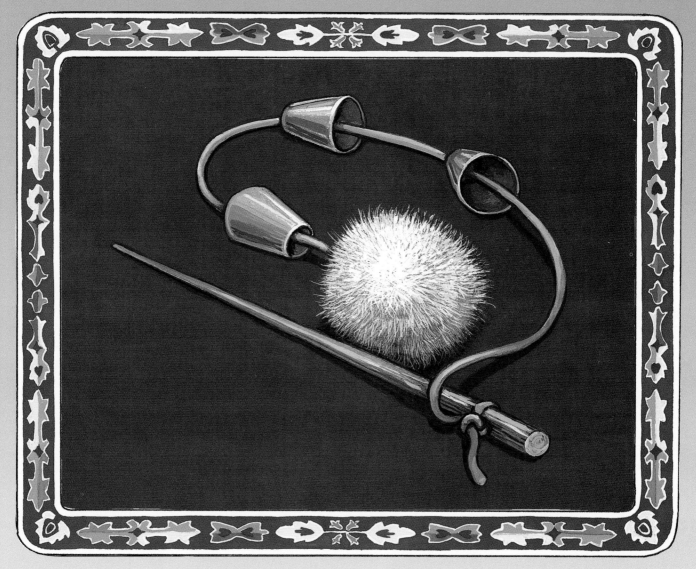

Third,

he tied the string to the stick.

Fourth,

he tried to catch the cones
on the end of the stick."

"And that," said grandmother, "is how the first kokolesh was made."

"Grandmother,"

said Mollie.

"I can make a kokolesh, too, from the things on the table!

I will use twine and sticks, cotton balls, and cake-decorating cones."

"And me, too!" said William.

26

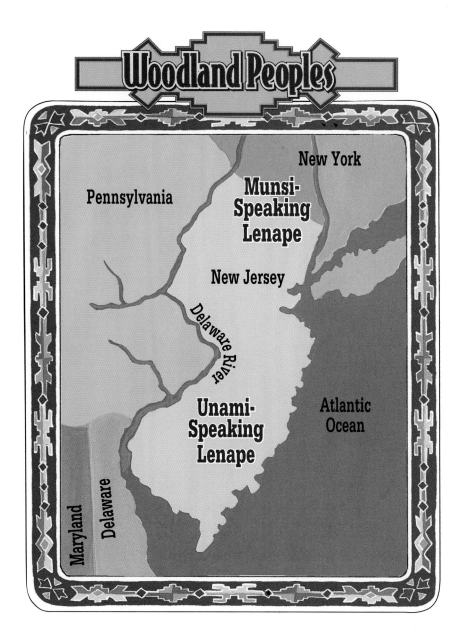

Long ago, the Lenape, or Delaware Indians, lived in the eastern part of the United States in an area we know as the states of New Jersey, New York, Eastern Pennsylvania, and Northern Delaware. The Munsi-speaking Lenape lived in the Northern third of New Jersey and surrounding areas of New York State. The Unami-speaking Lenape lived south of the Munsi-speakers. They had three clans: the Wolf, the Turkey, and the Turtle. Today, the Lenape live mostly in Oklahoma and Canada.

Storytelling

For Native Americans, storytelling has always been an important way of communicating history and traditions. Stories are told and retold to enable children to grasp their meaning and to help them understand and practice the family and tribal values being transmitted. Care is taken to acknowledge from whom a story was learned. This generational linking, along with giving credit, are important Native American values. They bind the family together and build respect for those who came before.

Traditionally, stories were told mainly during the winter months when a lot of time was spent inside lodges. At this time, children learned valuable lessons from listening to the stories elders told; from acting out and retelling the stories; and from playing and inventing games related to them.

Today, stories are told throughout the year. The focus remains on strengthening children's listening skills, but there is more attention given to listening for voice inflection, pauses, and emphasis while thinking about the storyline and the content. Although traditional storytelling and respect for the old ways are admired, ingenuity is encouraged. Woodland People take pride in their ability to adapt.

Making a Kokolesh

Here is a simple way to make a game for children of all ages that will develop hand-eye coordination and encourage competitive fun.

1. Measure off about 20 inches of leather string or strong twine.
2. Tie one end of the string or twine around a large cotton ball.
3. Cut off the narrow tips of three cake-decorating funnels.
    Be certain the stick fits through the hole of each cone.
4. String the funnels onto the string or twine, making certain the wide end of the cone is away from the cotton ball.
5. Using a pencil sharpener, sharpen one end of a dowel or stick, which is about 12 inches long.
6. Tie the other end of the string or twine around the unsharpened end of the stick. Make certain the string will not slide off the stick.
7. Holding the stick with the pointed end toward you, flick your wrist so the pointed end of the stick is moved away from your body and the cones on the string fly out.
8. Immediately try to spear the cones with the pointed end of the stick.
9. Keep a count of how well you do for three tries.
10. If you play with someone else, decide before you begin how many catches you need to win. Give a point for each cone that is speared.

This game can be adapted to children of various ages. For the younger child, use a larger stick and cone. Use a larger cotton wad at the end. One cone can be used instead of three. For older children, the challenge can be increased by using a smaller size stick, smaller cones, and three cones on the string. Rules can vary, such as having to catch all three cones in one try to get points.

About the Author

Rita Kohn grew up in the Catskill Mountains, went to college in
Buffalo, New York, and now calls both Illinois and Indiana home.
All these places are part of the ancestral territory of the
Woodland People. A lifelong love of the land and the People whose
spirit continues to give energy to these mountains, valleys, streams,
lakes, and fields leads her to listen, watch, and learn.
Her book is one way of continuing the circle of life.

About the Illustrator

Dorothy Sullivan, a member of the Cherokee Nation, is from
Norman, Oklahoma. Her love of western and Native American history
expresses itself in richly colored, well researched paintings depicting
authentic Cherokee heritage of the Eastern Band of North Carolina
and the Western Band of Oklahoma. Twenty-two signed and
numbered limited edition prints of her work are available in her
book *Cherokee Heritage Collection*. Ms. Sullivan's paintings
also have been included in the 1992 through 1995
"American Indian Art Calendar." Dorothy Sullivan is the mother
of five sons and one daughter and grandmother of nine grandchildren.
She taught art in the public schools for nineteen years and also worked
as a commercial artist and "quick draw" artist for newspapers.